MORRIS'S DISAPPEARING BAG

A CHRISTMAS STORY *by*

ROSEMARY WELLS

NEW YORK THE DIAL PRESS

a pied piper book

A Pied Piper Book
is a registered trademark of The Dial Press.
MORRIS'S DISAPPEARING BAG
is published in a hardcover edition by
The Dial Press,
1 Dag Hammarskjold Plaza,
New York, New York 10017.

ISBN 0-8037-5509-0

TO VICTORIA

It was Christmas morning.
"Wow!" said Morris.

Morris's brother, Victor,
got a hockey outfit.

Morris's sister, Rose,
got a beauty kit.

Morris's other sister, Betty,
got a chemistry set.

And Morris got a bear.

All Christmas day Victor played hockey
and Rose made herself beautiful
and Betty mixed acids.

And then Betty made herself beautiful
and Victor sorted test tubes
and Rose played left wing.

And then Victor made himself beautiful
and Betty played goalie
and Rose invented a new gas.

Morris was too young to play
with chemicals, said Betty,
he might blow up the house.

He was too little to play hockey,
said Victor, he might get hurt.

And he was too silly to use the
beauty kit, said Rose, he would
waste all the lipstick.

Nobody wanted Morris's bear.

"Come," said Morris's mother,
"let's make a hat for your bear."

"No!" said Morris.

"Let's take your bear for a walk,"
suggested Morris's father.
"No!" said Morris.

Morris wouldn't eat his dinner.
"What's the matter with Morris?" asked
   his father.
"I think he hit himself with the hockey
   puck," said Victor.

"Maybe he ate the lipstick," said Rose.
"It was the gas," said Betty.
"He breathed it in."

Morris sat under the Christmas tree.

Suddenly he noticed a package that
had been overlooked.

He opened it.
In it was a Disappearing Bag.

Morris crawled right in.

"Morris?" said Victor.
"Right here," said Morris.
"Where?" asked Victor.

"Where's Morris?" asked Betty and Rose.
"Over here," said Morris.

But they couldn't find him.
"Maybe he blew himself up," said Betty.

"Do you suppose he's so beautiful we
wouldn't recognize him?" asked Rose.
"Dad!" shouted Victor, "Morris is
skating so fast we can't see him."

Morris came out of his bag.
"Where were you?" asked Victor.
"I was in my Disappearing Bag,"
said Morris.

"I want to use it," shouted Victor.
"Me first," said Rose.
"You can use my chemicals," said Betty.

Morris held open his bag.
Everybody disappeared at once.

Then he zoomed

and mixed

and beautified

until bedtime.

"Bedtime!" said Morris.

"May I use the bag tomorrow?"
    asked Rose.
"I want to sleep in it tonight,"
    said Betty.

"Morris," said Victor, "I hope you
remember where you put the bag."

But Morris was already fast asleep.